The Ruby Princess Sees a Ghost

THE JEWEL KINGDOM

The Ruby Princess Sees a Ghost

JAHNNA N. MALCOLM

Illustrations by Neal McPheeters

SCHOLASTIC INC.
NEW YORK   TORONTO   LONDON   AUCKLAND   SYDNEY

ISBN 0-590-11713-0

Text copyright © 1997 by Jahnna Beecham and Malcolm Hillgartner.
All rights reserved. Published by Scholastic Inc.
LITTLE APPLE PAPERBACKS is a trademark of Scholastic Inc.

12 11 10 9 8 7 6 5 4 3 2 1   7 8 9/9 0 1 2/0

Printed in the U.S.A.   40
First Scholastic printing, November 1997

Designed by Elizabeth B. Parisi

For Nadine, baby Emma Rose,
and
Princess Katie Parker

CONTENTS

The Ruby Princess Sees a Ghost

THE JEWEL KINGDOM

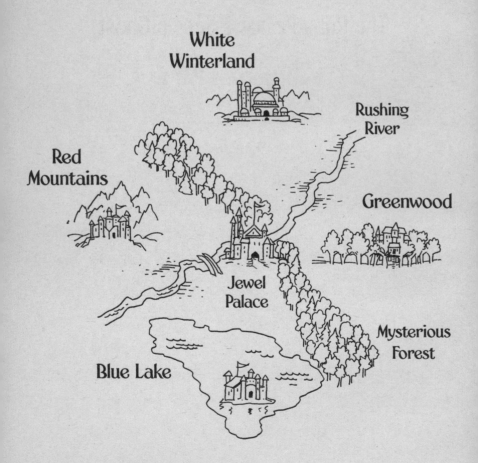

White
Winterland

Rushing
River

Red
Mountains

Greenwood

Jewel
Palace

Mysterious
Forest

Blue Lake

The Princess Party

 "I see them!" Roxanne cried. "My sisters are here!"

The Ruby Princess lifted the hem of her red gown. She leaped up the stone steps of her palace two at a time.

"Happy!" she called as she ran into the Great Hall. "The Jewel Princesses have arrived!"

A huge green Dragon with red-tipped

1

wings and clawed feet ducked his head into the hall. "What are you waiting for, my lady?" Hapgood asked. "Go and greet them!"

Roxanne swallowed hard. This was the first time her sisters or anyone had come to dinner at the Ruby Palace. It was a very important moment.

"Hapgood, I'm nervous," the princess confessed. "What if they don't like my palace?"

The Dragon lowered his huge head so that he was eye level with the princess. "Why wouldn't they like it?"

Roxanne shrugged. "Well, this palace is made of crumbling old stones. It can be very cold and drafty."

"All palaces are cold and drafty," Hapgood replied.

"Not my sister Sabrina's palace."

Roxanne thought the Sapphire Palace looked like a blue-and-white teacup. It floated on Blue Lake. And it was very sunny inside.

"What about the palace of the Emerald Princess?" Hapgood asked. "Doesn't it sit in the treetops? That has to be drafty."

"I'm sure the wind blows through the Greenwood," Roxanne said. "But the Emerald Palace is as cozy as a bird's nest."

Her sister's palace was a fun playhouse. Roxanne liked visiting Princess Emily because the Emerald Palace had lots of rope ladders and swings.

"Don't forget Princess Demetra," the Dragon added. "She lives in the White Winterland. Where there is always snow and ice."

It was true. Their parents, Queen

Jemma and King Regal, had given each of the sisters a land to rule. The Diamond Princess received the White Winterland. It was the coldest, snowiest place in the Jewel Kingdom. But Demetra loved living there.

"Demetra's palace is beautiful," Roxanne said with a sigh. "It's made out of crystal and it sparkles like a diamond in the snow."

Hapgood pointed to the palace windows. "Take a look at those Red Mountains out there. They are big and strong and full of mystery. Just like your Ruby Palace."

Roxanne folded her arms across her chest. "If my palace is so great, why won't anyone come here?"

"What do you mean?" the Dragon asked.

"I have asked many people from the Red Mountains to visit me. But not one of them has come to my palace."

"Maybe they're shy," Hapgood replied.

Roxanne shook her head. "No. They invite me to their homes. But they won't visit mine."

"That is something we need to look into," the Dragon said, scratching his neck with one clawed foot. "But for now, I must help Clove in the kitchen. And you must greet your sisters."

Roxanne's dark eyes widened. "Oh! I almost forgot."

She quickly fluffed out her thick, black hair. Then she fixed her silver crown and lifted her chin. "How do I look?"

"Every inch the Ruby Princess," Hapgood said with a bow. "Now go!"

The Dragon returned to the kitchen just as Roxanne's sisters reached the front door.

"Yoo-hoo!" the Emerald Princess called. "Anybody home?"

Roxanne saw her sister's curly red hair and cried, "Emily! I'm so glad you're here!"

Princess Emily was grinning from ear to ear as she hurried to hug Roxanne.

"Demetra and I raced each other from the front gate and I won," Emily whispered. "But don't tell her I told you!"

The Diamond Princess was right behind Emily. "I heard that!"

Emily wore a calf-length green skirt with a brown leather jacket and boots. She looked like she'd just come from a hike in the woods.

But Demetra seemed dressed for a fancy party. She wore a silver gown trimmed in sparkling diamonds. Silver ribbons were woven into her long, brown braid.

"Emily didn't win the race," Demetra said. "I did."

Princess Emily stuck her tongue out at Demetra. Demetra made a face back at Emily.

Roxanne giggled. It felt like old times, when they were growing up together at the Jewel Palace.

Sabrina, the Sapphire Princess, was the last to appear. Her flowing dress perfectly matched the color of her pale blue eyes. Sabrina's blond hair hung to her waist. She spoke in a soft voice.

"Sorry I'm late," Sabrina said as she hugged Roxanne. "I saw someone waving at me from the window."

"Which window?" Roxanne asked.

Sabrina went to the door and pointed at the tower. "That one."

"I'm the only one here," Roxanne said. "Except Hapgood and Clove the cook, and they're in the kitchen."

Emily whispered loudly, "Sabrina must be seeing things. She does that, you know."

Sabrina nudged Emily playfully. "That's not true, and you know it. I did see someone dressed all in white."

"But there's just me," Roxanne said with a frown. "And you can see, I'm not wearing white. My dress is red."

Emily's big green eyes widened. She turned to her sisters. "Then maybe it's true what they say."

"What?" Roxanne asked. "What do they say?"

"Haven't you heard?" Demetra asked

Roxanne. "Everyone in the Jewel Kingdom has been talking about it."

Roxanne was very confused. "Talking about what?"

"Your palace," Sabrina replied.

"But what do they *say* about my palace?" Roxanne asked.

Sabrina looked at Demetra. Demetra looked at Emily. Then the three sisters looked at Roxanne.

"It's haunted."

The Palace Is Haunted!

"My palace is not haunted!" Roxanne stamped her foot. "That is a very mean thing to say."

"We didn't say it to be mean," Sabrina explained. "We're just telling you what we've heard."

"I would know if my palace had a ghost," Roxanne said. "I'd hear things, wouldn't I?"

"Like chains," Emily said in a spooky voice. "Ghosts always rattle chains."

"And you'd probably see things, too," Princess Demetra added. "Like floating chairs."

"I've heard that it feels very cold when you are near a ghost," Sabrina said, shivering a little.

"Have you felt cold? Or heard chains? Or seen floating chairs?" Emily asked.

Princess Roxanne tried to think. Her palace *was* cold. And she did hear things. Like a door creaking. Or tree limbs tapping against the windows. But those didn't seem like ghost sounds. And she knew she'd never seen anything float. Especially not a chair.

"I'm positive I don't have a ghost," Roxanne finally said.

At that instant the sisters heard a loud scream.

A large Craghopper galloped into the room. She was a goatlike creature with big horns and hooves. She wore an apron and carried a wooden spoon.

"Clove, what's the matter?" Roxanne asked the cook.

Clove spun in a circle, confused. "I saw it with my own eyes," she said. "Big as life. Floating in my kitchen."

"Saw what?" Roxanne asked.

But Clove didn't answer her. She ran out the front door of the palace.

Before the princesses could say a word, another creature appeared. It was a big green Dragon. He also wore an apron.

"Clove, wait!" Hapgood shouted in his deep voice. "I'll take you home."

The Dragon bowed to the four princesses. "Forgive me, ladies," Hapgood said. "But the cook and I have just seen a ghost."

"A ghost!" Princess Demetra gasped. "Where is it?"

"In the kitchen!" Hapgood called as he hurried out the front door of the Ruby Palace. Then he spread his wings and was gone.

"There can't be a ghost!" Roxanne announced. "This must be some kind of joke."

"Did you see Clove's face?" Sabrina asked. "She didn't look like she was joking. She was scared."

Demetra turned toward the kitchen. "I'm feeling a little scared myself."

Roxanne was upset. Not about the ghost. But about her party. If her sisters were afraid of her palace, the party would be ruined.

"Now everyone stay calm," Roxanne ordered. "Clove is a very jumpy Craghopper. She's afraid of her own shadow. Last week Clove thought she saw a mouse and she hopped right out the window."

"But what about Hapgood?" Emily asked. "He said he saw a ghost, too."

"He just said that to make Clove feel better." Roxanne put her hands on her hips. "Believe me. There is no ghost."

Demetra wasn't so sure. She folded her arms across her chest and said, "Prove it."

"How?" Roxanne asked.

Demetra pointed to the far door. "Go in the kitchen."

Roxanne looked Demetra straight in the eye. "All right. I will."

She marched across the Great Hall into the kitchen.

"Roxanne, be careful!" Sabrina called after her.

In the kitchen, Roxanne saw a kettle of

stew boiling over in the fireplace. From the stone oven came the delicious smell of baked bread. An unfinished royalberry pie was still on the cutting board. But there was no sign of anything odd.

"I knew there wasn't a ghost," Roxanne said. She took the bread out of the oven and pulled the stew from the fire so they wouldn't burn.

The princess was about to leave the kitchen when she saw something white. It was next to the back door.

Roxanne covered her mouth and tried not to scream. She waited for the ghost to fly up and scare her. But it didn't move.

The Ruby Princess forced herself to walk toward the white thing. Maybe she could scare it away.

But the closer she got, the more she

could see it. Finally she cried, "That's no ghost. It's just Clove's apron."

Roxanne grabbed the apron. Then she ran back to join her sisters. "There was no ghost, just this apron."

"How can you be sure there's no ghost?" Demetra asked.

"Because this is my home," Roxanne answered. "I've never heard or seen anything unusual since the day I moved in."

"Th-th-then what's *that*?" Emily squeaked, pointing to the front hall.

A white shape floated in midair.

Demetra clutched Sabrina's hand and whispered, "I don't like this. I don't like it at all."

"Me, neither," Sabrina said in a very shaky voice.

Roxanne stared in amazement. The

white shape looked like a ghost. But was it really a ghost? She reached out her hand to touch it.

The ghost flew up the stairs. Seconds later, a picture fell off the wall.

Ha! Ha! Ha! Ha!

Eerie laughter echoed down the stairwell.

Demetra buried her head in Sabrina's shoulder and cried, "I want to go home!"

The Party's Over

———✦———

 "Please don't go," Princess Roxanne begged Demetra. "That won't happen again. I'm sure of it."

Thump, drag. Thump, drag.

Roxanne looked up at the ceiling. Something was being dragged across the floor above them. "I don't understand," she mumbled.

"What is there to understand?" Emily

hissed. "You have a ghost and that's all there is to it!"

Thump, drag. Thump, drag.

The sound was much louder.

Demetra turned to her sisters. "I don't know about you but I'm not staying here another —"

Before Demetra could finish her sentence, something whooshed by the window and stopped outside the palace door.

The princesses watched in terror as the great wooden door creaked open.

A puff of smoke came into the hall, followed by a large green head.

"Happy!" Roxanne ran to hug the Dragon. "You came back!"

"I'm sorry to have left you like that," Hapgood said, "but Clove was so upset, I had to take her home immediately."

"OOOOOOOOOooooo!" A loud moan came from upstairs.

"That's it!" Demetra's face was white as a sheet. "I'm going home."

"I'm with you!" Emily shouted.

Both girls ran to the Dragon. "Hapgood, fly us away from that ghost. Please!"

Hapgood bowed his head. "Of course, my ladies."

Demetra and Emily quickly climbed onto the Dragon's back. Roxanne was disappointed that two of her sisters were leaving, but she was glad that Sabrina was staying.

"Too bad for them," Roxanne said to the Sapphire Princess. "They're going to miss out on a very fun dinner."

Sabrina looked at Roxanne. Then she looked at the stone floor. "Roxanne . . ."

"Oh, no," Roxanne groaned. "Not you, too."

Sabrina took both of Roxanne's hands in hers. "We wouldn't have any fun if I stayed. I would be too scared. We'll all come back another time."

"Roxanne, you should come with us," Emily called.

"Yes!" Demetra cried. "You can't stay here with that ghost. It isn't safe."

Roxanne wasn't afraid of being alone. Why should she be? There had to be a logical explanation for what they'd seen and heard. It couldn't be a ghost.

"This is my palace," Roxanne said firmly. "I'm staying put."

Hapgood cleared his throat. "Are you sure you'll be all right by yourself, Princess?"

"I'll be fine," Roxanne said, patting the

23

Dragon's neck. "Now take my sisters home and fly carefully."

Hapgood nodded his head. "Yes, my lady."

Sabrina joined her sisters on Hapgood's back. The dragon strode into the palace courtyard.

Sabrina waved farewell. "I'm sorry your party was spoiled," she called.

"I'm sorry, too," Roxanne replied. "Please come back soon."

Hapgood flapped his mighty wings and rose into the evening sky. The Ruby Princess watched until they had flown out of sight. Then she sadly returned to her palace.

Roxanne thought she was alone. But the second she shut the front door, a voice whispered, "Now it's just you and me."

4

Follow That Ghost!

There *was* a ghost in the Ruby Palace! And it was coming to get her!

The Ruby Princess slowly backed away from the ghost. She wanted to run and hide. But how do you hide from a ghost? Couldn't they fly and walk through walls?

"Run, little princess!" the ghost hissed, swooping closer. "Run!"

Roxanne tripped over a bench by the front door. She fell back against the stone wall. Her hand slammed into the red-and-silver shield that hung on the wall.

"My shield!" she whispered. "I'll use my magic shield."

The magic shield was a gift from the great wizard Gallivant. It had the power to make her invisible. Maybe if the ghost couldn't see her, she could escape.

"I'm going to get you!" the ghost threatened.

Roxanne hid against the wall. Her hand shook as she raised the shield in front of her. She began to chant, *"Oh, magic shield —"*

Clink!

Something dropped on the floor and rolled toward her.

"Oh, no!" the ghost cried out.

It bent to grab the round, shiny object, but Roxanne got there first.

"What's this?" the princess murmured. "A ring?"

"Argh!" growled the ghost. Then it disappeared up the stairs.

"Wait!" Roxanne shouted.

She followed the ghost to the second floor of the palace. As she did, she looked at the ring. Roxanne had never seen anything like it before. A royal crest was carved on it. But it wasn't the crest of her father, King Regal. And there was an odd stone in the center. A black stone.

Roxanne looked up. She had reached the tower room. But where was the ghost?

Could it have flown out the high window? Could it have turned around and passed her in the hall? She didn't think so.

Roxanne listened for a sound. Any sound.

After a few seconds, she heard something. A crunching sound, like feet walking on gravel. It seemed to be coming from behind the tower wall. Roxanne stared at the red stones for a long time. Finally she saw a familiar outline. "I see it," she gasped. "A secret door! . . ."

The door was just tall enough for a small person to slip through.

"But how do you open it?" Roxanne murmured. She tried to fit her fingernails in the crack. Then she patted the stones around the door, feeling for a knob or key.

"This stone is loose," she said, wiggling one on the side of the door.

The Ruby Princess gave the stone a tug. Suddenly the door swung open. Cold

air whooshed into the room. With it came a bad smell, like an old cellar.

"Ugh!" Roxanne covered her nose and peered into the opening. A narrow staircase circled down into the darkness. She could hear the echo of footsteps far away.

"I have to follow that ghost," she declared. Roxanne tightened her grip on her shield. "I'd better do it now while I have the courage."

She was halfway through the tiny door when a voice behind her cried out, "Don't move!"

The Secret Door

"Sabrina!" Roxanne gasped as she turned around. "You scared me to death!"

Princess Sabrina ran to Roxanne and hugged her. "I couldn't bear to leave you all by yourself in this scary old palace. Hapgood brought me back. Then I heard a noise coming from up here and I followed it."

Roxanne smiled at her sister. "That was very brave of you."

"I'm not nearly as brave as you," Sabrina replied. She pointed at the secret door. "Were you really going to go in there by yourself?"

Roxanne pulled Sabrina away from the door. "I saw the ghost," she whispered, "and was about to run when something odd happened. The ghost dropped this ring."

Roxanne showed Sabrina the gold ring with the strange crest and black stone.

"Oh, my!" Sabrina gasped.

"What's the matter?" Roxanne asked.

"I know that crest," Sabrina said in a hushed voice. "It belongs to Lord Bleak."

"Lord Bleak!" Roxanne whispered. "Oh, no!"

Lord Bleak was a terrible man. He ruled the Jewel Kingdom before they were born. Those years were called the Dark Times. When their parents became king and queen of the Jewel Kingdom, Lord Bleak was sent far away. Now he lived across the Black Sea and had been told to never return.

"Are you sure this crest is Lord Bleak's?" Roxanne asked.

"Positive," Sabrina replied. "Do you remember when we were little and we sneaked into the cellar of the Jewel Palace?"

Roxanne remembered it well. The girls had been forbidden to go down there by their parents. But they went anyway. And they found weapons and pictures from the Dark Times.

"There was a black shield, and on it was

this crest." Sabrina pointed to the ring. "See? It's the same. The snake and the skull."

Roxanne held the ring away from her. "That explains the bad feeling I get when I look at this ring."

"But why would a ghost have this ring?" Sabrina asked. "I don't understand."

"Maybe Lord Bleak sent this ghost to us," Roxanne replied. "Maybe he *wanted* us to know he sent the ghost."

Roxanne frowned. "But why would it come through that door? I thought ghosts could walk through walls."

Sabrina tiptoed closer and peeked into the darkness. "Where do you think those stairs lead?"

"I don't know," Roxanne replied. "But I think we'd better find out."

Sabrina's eyes widened. "We?"

"You're coming with me, aren't you?"

Roxanne didn't feel as brave as she had before. Talking about Lord Bleak made her scared. "I can't go into the dark alone. I need your help."

Sabrina took a deep breath. "When you put it that way, I guess I have to go with you."

The sisters took two candlesticks and lit them.

Sabrina held her candle up to the secret door. "Do you want to go first?" she asked in a shaky voice.

"No," Roxanne answered with the same shakiness. "I think we should go down together."

The Ruby Princess held hands with the Sapphire Princess. And together, they stepped into the secret passage.

Into the Mysterious Forest

The steps seemed to go down forever. When the princesses finally reached the bottom, they found themselves in a damp tunnel. Pools of muddy water dotted the floor.

"I think we're far below the castle," Roxanne whispered, trying not to step in the puddles.

The two sisters followed the tunnel for

a long way. At last they came to another set of steps. These were made of dirt and they led up to a small cave.

"That cave must lead to the outside," Roxanne cried, running up the steps. "I can see light. Let's go see where we are."

"Roxanne, slow down!" Sabrina called, clutching the back of her sister's gown. "Something terrible could be waiting outside to grab us."

Roxanne knew Sabrina was right. At the top of the steps, she flattened herself against the stone wall. Then she slowly inched her way to the cave opening and peeked outside.

Twisted black trees surrounded the cave. Bushes with wicked thorns covered the ground. Roxanne knew just where they were.

"Oh, Sabrina!" she cried. "We've come

to an awful place. This is the Mysterious Forest."

Sabrina covered her mouth, trying not to scream. The Mysterious Forest cut across the Jewel Kingdom. It looked like a big black shadow. From the time the princesses were little, they had been warned never to go there. Bad things happened in those woods.

"Roxanne, let's go back!" Sabrina tugged on her sister's sleeve. "Before it's too late."

Roxanne wanted to turn and run, too. But something stopped her. Voices. Darklings. Just ahead.

Roxanne put a finger to her lips and motioned for Sabrina to follow her. The Sapphire Princess started to protest, but Roxanne grabbed her hand and pulled her forward.

Thorns tore at their gowns. Snaky vines dropped from the branches and blocked their way. Roxanne held her shield in front of her and pushed through the brush.

Soon the Jewel Princesses came to a small clearing. Two figures were sitting on a rotting log by a campfire. Both were laughing so hard, they could barely talk.

Roxanne didn't know who they were, but she recognized their outfits. They were dressed in black capes with big black hoods.

"Darklings," she murmured. "What are they doing here?"

Darklings were Lord Bleak's people. They wore hooded capes that hid their faces from the rest of the world.

Roxanne heard that Darklings had

once been very handsome. But the evil inside them was so strong that it twisted their faces. Now they were as ugly on the outside as they were on the inside.

"They must be royalty," Sabrina whispered. "Look. They have Lord Bleak's Snake-and-Skull crest on their capes."

"This is not good," Roxanne said, shaking her head slowly. "Not good at all."

Roxanne and Sabrina crept forward and knelt down in the weeds near the log.

"Did you see the look on those stupid princesses' faces when the painting fell off the wall?" the tallest Darkling asked.

Her friend snorted, "They were scared out of their wits!"

Suddenly a white figure stepped out from behind the tree.

"The ghost!" Sabrina squeaked.

Roxanne covered her sister's mouth

with one hand and stared at the white figure. Something wasn't right.

"The cook nearly cut off her hoof when she saw you," the short Darkling said to the ghost.

"Even the Dragon was scared," the other Darkling laughed.

The ghost bent over at the waist, laughing, too. Roxanne saw the hem of a dress at the ghost's ankles. And below the dress were black pointy-toed shoes.

Roxanne nudged Sabrina and pointed to the shoes. Sabrina cocked her head, confused. What kind of ghost wore shoes?

"One more night like tonight and the Ruby Princess will leave her palace for good," the tall Darkling snickered.

"Then the people of the Red Mountains will know they made a

mistake!" the ghost declared. "They'll think Roxanne is a rotten princess."

"And you will have your revenge!" the tall Darkling screeched.

"Yes!"

The ghost suddenly grabbed the top of its head and pulled. A white sheet slipped to the ground. Underneath the sheet was a dark-haired girl with twisted, scarred features.

"Th-that's no ghost," Sabrina gasped. "That's a girl!"

"And not just any girl," Roxanne said grimly. "That's Lord Bleak's daughter. The terrible Princess Rudgrin!"

Boo to You!

———◆◆◆———

Roxanne and Sabrina raced back to the cave. They needed to talk.

"I can't believe that Princess Rudgrin would play such a mean trick on us!" Sabrina huffed, trying to catch her breath.

"I believe it," Roxanne said with a frown. "Remember what happened at our coronation? She tried to take my place and be crowned the Ruby Princess."

"But you stopped her." Sabrina looked back at the clearing. "Now Princess Rudgrin is trying to get back at you by scaring you out of your palace."

Roxanne put one hand on her hip. "I'll never move out. Ever!"

"What do you think we should do?"

Roxanne paced in a small circle. "Rudgrin and her friends tried to frighten us," she said, thinking hard. "Maybe we should do the same to them."

"How?" Sabrina asked. "Dress up as ghosts and chase them?"

"But what would we wear?" Roxanne drummed her fingers on her shield. "We have to think of something else."

Sabrina twisted a strand of her long

blond hair. "I guess the only thing scarier than seeing a ghost is *not* seeing a ghost."

Roxanne stopped drumming her fingers. "What do you mean?"

"Real ghosts are invisible. They make things float in the air."

"Of course!" Roxanne's eyes lit up. "Sabrina! You're a genius!" She gave her sister a big bear hug.

"What did I say?" Sabrina asked.

"You said ghosts are invisible!" Roxanne could barely keep from shouting. "Well, *we* can be invisible, too. And we can make things float in the air."

"How can we be invisible?" Sabrina whispered.

"With this." Roxanne raised her red-and-silver shield. "I just have to say the magic words and we'll disappear."

"I know your shield can make disappear," Sabrina said. "But what about me?"

"All you have to do is hold my hand. As long as you are touching me, you will be invisible, too."

"I can do that." Sabrina held out her hand and Roxanne grasped it tightly.

Then Roxanne held the magic shield in front of them both and chanted, *"Oh, Magic Shield with power so bright, hide us from all others' sight."*

"Am I invisible?" Sabrina whispered as they made their way back to the campfire. "I don't feel invisible."

"You are," Roxanne whispered back. "Trust me."

When they reached the campfire, Princess Rudgrin and her friends were still hooting with laughter.

"Come on." Roxanne squeezed Sabrina's hand. "Let's go get them!"

Sabrina and Roxanne tiptoed up behind Princess Rudgrin. Roxanne took a deep breath and blew in Rudgrin's ear.

Rudgrin batted at her ear with one hand. Roxanne blew again. Rudgrin shook her head and scratched her ear.

"These awful bugs!" Rudgrin grumbled, as Roxanne made a buzzing sound. "Get them away from me."

Then Sabrina tugged at the back of Rudgrin's dress.

Rudgrin spun to face the tall Darkling. "Why did you do that?"

"Do what?" the Darkling asked.

Rudgrin scowled. "You pulled my dress. Don't deny it."

"I did not!" the Darkling snapped.

Roxanne tugged on the other side of

Rudgrin's dress. Rudgrin spun around to face the other Darkling. "Now *you* pulled my dress."

The Darkling folded her arms across her chest and said, "I did not."

Roxanne and Sabrina circled the three girls, pulling their hair, tugging their dresses, and pinching them on the arms.

"Yeow! Stop that!" Princess Rudgrin screeched. She grabbed the Darklings by the hair and yanked very hard.

Soon all three of them were rolling on the ground, hitting and scratching one another. They looked so silly that Roxanne and Sabrina almost burst out laughing.

Then Roxanne and Sabrina picked up rocks around the campfire and tossed them in the air.

"Look!" the tall Darkling gasped. "Those rocks are alive."

"That's impossible," Rudgrin growled.

Roxanne swooped her rock through the air and dropped it on Rudgrin's foot.

"Yeow!" Rudgrin screamed. She punched the Darkling in the shoulder. "Why did you do that to me?"

"I didn't do a thing," the Darkling answered. "I swear."

Sabrina placed her rock in the tall Darkling's hand.

"Then what's that rock doing in your hand?" Rudgrin demanded.

The Darkling quickly dropped the rock. But it was too late. Rudgrin was really angry. She picked up a stick and chased the Darkling around the campfire.

Sabrina found the white sheet lying on the ground. She waved it in front of the other Darkling. "Whoo-oo-oo!"

"I'm going to get you," Roxanne moaned in her best ghostly voice.

Rudgrin and the tall Darkling stopped running.

"That's a . . . that's a . . . *ghost!*" the short Darkling cried. "It has to be."

"Ru-ud-gr-i-i-nnnn!" Roxanne wailed. "You had better run!"

Suddenly Rudgrin's friends bolted away from the campfire. Sabrina, still waving the white sheet in the air, chased after them.

"Wait! You let go of my hand!" Roxanne shouted to her sister.

The Sapphire Princess had just reached the edge of the forest. She froze and looked down at her blue flowing gown and sapphire cape.

"Oh, no," Sabrina groaned, "Princess Rudgrin can see me!"

Good-bye, Ghost!

Now they were in trouble!

Roxanne was still invisible, but not Sabrina.

"Why, if it isn't the Sapphire Princess," Rudgrin said in a very cold voice. "So you were the one scaring my friends."

"And you were trying to scare my sister," Sabrina said, pretending she was alone. "But it didn't work."

Roxanne stepped quietly between Rudgrin and Sabrina. If the Darkling Princess tried to do something mean to her sister, Roxanne could stop her.

"Everyone in the Red Mountains thinks Roxanne's palace is haunted," Rudgrin sneered. "Now no one will *ever* come to visit her."

Rudgrin's words made Roxanne mad. She wanted to punch Rudgrin in the nose. But she knew that wouldn't solve anything.

"Your sister won't have any friends," Princess Rudgrin continued. "Soon she'll be so lonely she'll go running home to Mommy and Daddy."

Roxanne yelled in Rudgrin's face, "*Wrong!*"

This startled Princess Rudgrin so much, she stumbled backward and fell on the ground.

Roxanne hadn't meant to give herself away but she couldn't help herself.

"You coward," she shouted at Rudgrin. "You don't have the courage to face me in person. You have to sneak into my palace and pretend to be a ghost."

Princess Rudgrin twisted in every direction, looking for the owner of the voice. "Who are you?" she rasped. "Where are you?"

"I'm right here!" Roxanne dropped her shield to the ground. At once she was visible again.

Rudgrin saw her and gasped.

Roxanne announced in her most regal voice, "I am Roxanne, the Ruby Princess, Ruler of the Red Mountains. And I know who you are." Roxanne pointed at Rudgrin. "You're just a mean little girl hiding under a sheet!"

Sabrina hurried to Roxanne's side. "That's telling her, sister."

"Now I want you to leave the Jewel Kingdom and never return," Roxanne finished.

Rudgrin had been very scared. But once she saw that the ghostly voice belonged to Roxanne, her courage came back. She stood up.

"I'm not leaving." Rudgrin folded her arms across her chest. "And you can't make me."

Roxanne opened her mouth to speak, but another voice spoke first. "Maybe I can."

Rudgrin was staring at something behind Roxanne. Her jaw opened and shut but she couldn't make a sound.

Sabrina and Roxanne slowly turned.

A young girl in a long velvet dress with

fur trim floated two feet above the ground. A lace veil trailed behind her pointed hat.

There was no doubt about it. This was a *real* ghost.

The ghost drifted over to Rudgrin. She leaned forward and, in a very soft voice, said, "Boo!

Rudgrin ran screaming into the woods.

The ghost followed her. "You tell that dreadful Lord Bleak that Lady Lucy sent you home," she cried. "Tell him if he ever lets you back in the Jewel Kingdom, I will come to your castle and haunt your family forever mo-oo-oo-oo-oo-re!"

The ghost held out the last word. Then she winked at Roxanne, and vanished.

The princesses stood in the clearing for a very long time before either of them spoke.

Finally Roxanne turned to Sabrina. "Did we really see what I think we saw?" she asked.

Sabrina nodded slowly. "Yes. A little ghost named Lady Lucy suddenly appeared out of nowhere and told Princess Rudgrin to go home."

"Lucy . . . Lucy . . ." Roxanne repeated the name to herself. "I think her portrait hangs above the stairs in the Ruby Palace."

"I thought she looked familiar," Sabrina said. "That's the painting that Rudgrin dropped, trying to scare us. Dropping it must have disturbed Lucy's spirit!"

Roxanne burst out laughing.

"What's so funny?" Sabrina asked.

"It looks like Rudgrin's dirty trick came back to haunt her!" Roxanne giggled. Then she took Sabrina's hand and said, "Come on. Let's go home."

Before they left the Mysterious Forest, Roxanne made sure they blocked the cave entrance. The two princesses rolled several large boulders in front of the cave. Then they piled broken tree branches on top of the rocks.

"That should stop any pretend ghosts from sneaking into my palace," Roxanne said when they'd finished.

Just then they heard a loud whoosh over their heads. It was followed by the flapping of wings.

Both girls looked up. Above the treetops was the dark outline of a Dragon. Two figures rode on its back.

"Hapgood?" Roxanne shouted toward the sky. "Is that you?"

"Roxanne!" Emily's voice echoed in the darkness. "I heard Roxanne! Go back, Happy!"

"It's Hapgood," Roxanne cried with delight. "He's come looking for us."

"Our sisters are still with him," Sabrina said as they watched the Dragon circle back and look for a place to land.

Roxanne and Sabrina ran to the edge of the Mysterious Forest. "We're over here," they shouted. "By the meadow."

The Dragon swooped in front of them and gently touched down. Before he could even fold his wings, Demetra and Emily were off his back and running toward Roxanne and Sabrina.

"We went back to the palace and you were both gone!" Emily cried. "We were so worried!"

"Are you all right?" Demetra asked. "Did that ghost hurt you?"

"Which ghost?" Roxanne asked.

"You mean there's more than one?" Demetra gasped.

"Roxanne will tell you all about it," Sabrina cut in. "But not here. We should go back to the Ruby Palace."

"That's a capital idea," Hapgood said, joining the circle of princesses. "Why, we could even have dinner. The food is ready and waiting to be served."

Princess Emily licked her lips. "Now that you mention it, I'm starved."

Demetra nodded. "Me, too."

"Then let's go!" Roxanne cried. She was grinning so hard her cheeks hurt. Her party wasn't ruined after all.

The four princesses hopped onto Hapgood's back.

As the Dragon rose into the evening sky, Sabrina declared, "After dinner, Roxanne will tell us the story of how she battled an evil princess, frightened a fake ghost, and was saved by a real one. The amazing Lady Lucy of the Red Mountains."

The princesses heard a tiny voice cry with glee, "That's me!"

About the Authors

JAHNNA N. MALCOLM stands for Jahnna "and" Malcolm. Jahnna Beecham and Malcolm Hillgartner are married and write together. They have written over seventy books for kids. Jahnna N. Malcolm have written about ballerinas, horses, ghosts, singing cowgirls, and green slime.

Before Jahnna and Malcolm wrote books, they were actors. They met on the stage where Malcolm was playing a prince. And they were married on the stage where Jahnna was playing a princess.

Now they have their own little prince and princess: Dash and Skye. They all live in Ashland, Oregon, with their big red dog, Ruby, and their fluffy little white dog, Clarence.

A World of Dazzling Magic

THE JEWEL KINGDOM

With their special jewel powers, Sabrina, Demetra, Roxanne, and Emily rule the land and keep the unicorns, dragons, nymphs, and other wonderful creatures safe. Join them for adventure after adventure full of dazzling magic!

- ❑ BCF-21283-4 *1 Ruby Princess Runs Away* $3.99
- ❑ BCF-21284-2 *2 Sapphire Princess Meets a Monster* $3.99
- ❑ BCF-21287-7 *3 The Emerald Princess Plays a Trick* $3.99
- ❑ BCF-21289-3 *4 The Diamond Princess Saves The Day* $3.99
- ❑ BCF-11713-0 *5 The Ruby Princess Sees a Ghost* $3.99

Available wherever you buy books, or use this order form.